Piet Mondrian
Composition with Red Blue and Yellow

Louise Bourgeois
Spider

Kehinde Wiley

Vincent van Gogh
Still Life with Blue Enamel Coffeepot

Jeff Koons
Balloon Dog

Frank Gehry
Guggenheim Museum

Niki de Saint Phalle
Nana

For my mother who never stopped taking me to the museum!

Other books in the Princess Arabella series:

Princess Arabella's Birthday
Princess Arabella Mixes Colors
Princess Arabella and the Giant Cake
Princess Arabella Goes to School
Princess Arabella is a Big Sister

First published in the USA in 2020 by Cassava Republic Press
First published in Belgium by Uitgeverij De Eenhoorn

©Text and illustration: Mylo Freeman

Original Title: Prinses Arabella in het museum
©2019 Uitgeverij De Eenhoorn, Vlasstraat 17, B-8710 Wielsbeke

ISBN 978-1913175-06-1

A CIP catalogue record for this book is available from the British Library.

Printed and bound in the UK by Bell & Bain Ltd.

www.cassavarepublic.biz
www.mylofreeman.com

Mylo Freeman

Princess *Arabella* at the Museum

MARLENE DUMAS

GRAYSON PERRY

AIDA MULUNEH

KEHINDE WILEY

YAYOI KUSAMA

CASSAVA REPUBLIC

FEEDING THE AFRICAN IMAGINATION

Today, Princess Arabella and her friends are off to the museum.

Not just any museum...
But her very own Princess Arabella museum!

'And what are we going to do here?' asks Prince Mimoun.
'Look at beautiful things, of course!' Princess Arabella replies.
'My dad says that it's possible to disappear inside a painting,'
says Princess Ling.
'Is it possible to eat in a museum?' Princess Sofie wonders.
Suddenly everyone hears a loud shriek.
'Look, it's a monster!' Prince Jonas calls out.

In the big hall, a giant spider appears.
'But it's not a real spider, feel it,' says Princess Arabella.
The spider feels cold and hard.
'This sculpture is supposed to be a mother spider,'
Arabella explains.
'So that makes us her baby spiders,' Prince Jonas giggles.

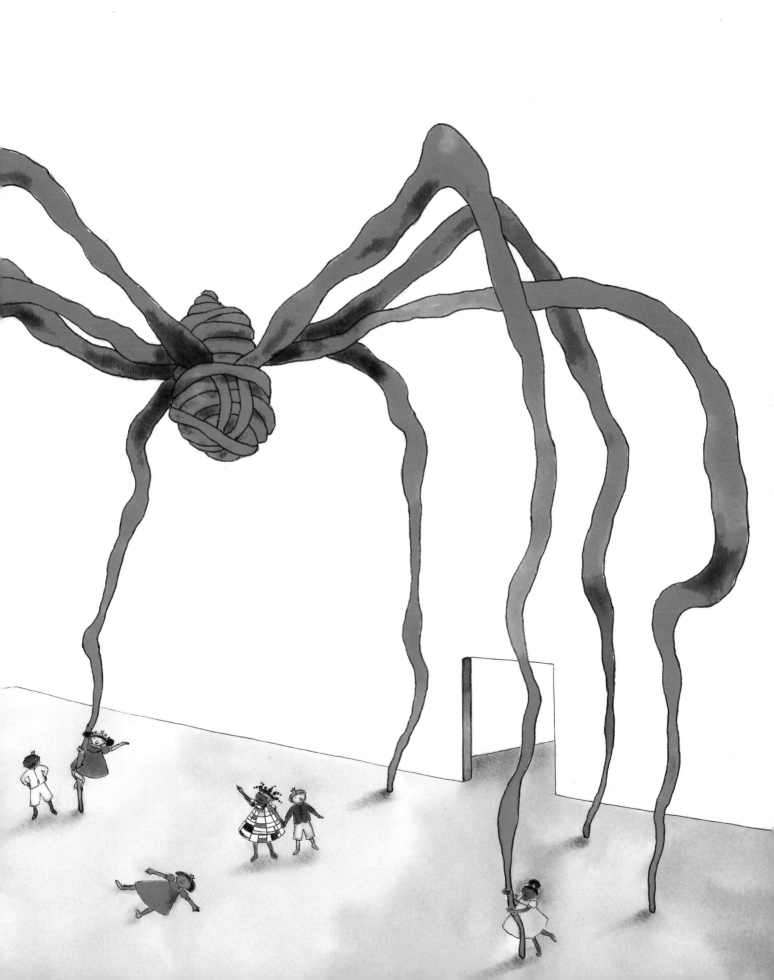

'Come and see,' says Prince Imani.
In this hall there are giant pumpkins.
'Adinda, how many dots can you count?'
Princess Adinda closes her eyes, but she can still see the dots.
In her mind, they are all sorts of different colors.
For a moment, it feels as if she is floating between the pumpkins.

In the next hall, there are even more statues.
'Look, I'm a statue too!' Prince Imani jokes.
'Me too!' laughs Princess Arabella.

Prince Jonas is standing so close to the painting, his nose almost touches it.

Then he takes a step back and looks again.

'Oh, your mom and dad look so real in this painting!' he whispers.

Princess Arabella feels so proud.

'Aren't they beautiful?'

'Why are there no flowers in these vases?'
Prince Milan asks.
'Every vase tells a story,' says Princess Arabella.
'Which vase do you like best? I like the one with the
elephants, of course!'

'Oh no! Those babies are far too big!'
Prince Mimoun calls out. 'How can anyone cuddle them?'
'Babies are supposed to be small,' says Princess Adinda.
'Look, just like my doll.'
'But sometimes they're supposed to be big!'
Princess Arabella giggles. 'Just look at the painting!'

'Why are you and your mom's faces blue?'
asks Prince Mimoun.
'I think it's strange,' says Princess Ling.
'I think it's magnificent!' says Prince Jonas.
'Green, blue, purple or red, I can still recognise both
of you,' Princess Naomi insists.

'**Arabella, look out! You're disappearing into the painting!**' shouts Prince Mimoun.

'I'm fine!' Princess Arabella laughs.

'This is my favorite painting of them all!'

But suddenly they hear a loud rumbling sound coming from the other hall...

It's Princess Sofie's tummy!
'This is not a real cake,' she moans.
'And I'm so hungry!'
'Don't worry,' says Princess Arabella. 'We're going to eat something really yummy.'

Princess Sofie takes a big bite out of her cupcake right away and takes a deep sigh. Prince Mimoun gobbles his cake really quickly and rubs his tummy.
'And now we can go home,' he says.

'Didn't you enjoy your visit to the museum?'
Princess Arabella asks, surprised.
'No, that's not it,' laughs Prince Mimoun.
'I've seen so many beautiful things.
Now I want to make a drawing of my own!'
And they all agree.

Alexandros of Antioch
Venus de Milo

Keith Haring
Untitled

Andy Warhol
Marilyn Monroe 31

Edgar Degas
Little Dancer Aged Fourteen

Leonardo da Vinci
The Last Supper

Claes Oldenburg
Floor Cake

Aida Muluneh
All in One

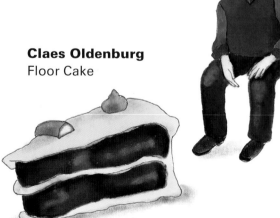